THIS WALKER BOOK BELONGS TO:

_____

_____

_____

_____

For Robert

First published 1994 by
Walker Books Ltd
87 Vauxhall Walk, London SE11 5HJ

This edition published 1995

6 8 10 9 7 5

© 1994 Nick Sharratt

This book has been typeset in Arial.

Printed in Hong Kong/China

British Library Cataloguing in Publication Data
A catalogue record for this book is
available from the British Library.

ISBN 0-7445-4307-X

My Mum and Dad Make Me Laugh

Nick Sharratt

WALKER BOOKS

AND SUBSIDIARIES

LONDON • BOSTON • SYDNEY

My mum and dad make me laugh.

One likes spots and the other likes stripes.

My mum likes spots in winter

and spots in summer.

DOT TO DOT
PUZZLES

My dad likes stripes on weekdays

and stripes at weekends.

Last weekend we went to the safari park. My mum put on her spottiest dress and earrings, and my dad put on his stripiest suit and tie.

I put on my grey top and trousers.
"You do like funny clothes!" said my mum and dad.

We set off in the car and on the way we stopped for something to eat.
My mum had a spotty pizza and my dad had a stripy ice cream.

I had a bun. "You do like funny food!" said my mum and dad.

When we got to the safari park it was very exciting.
My mum liked the big cats best.

"Those are splendid spots," she said. "And I should know!"

My dad liked the zebras best.

"Those are super stripes," he said. "And I should know!"

But the animals I liked best didn't have spots and didn't have stripes.
They were big and grey and eating their tea.

"Those are really good elephants," I said.

"And I should know!"

MORE WALKER PAPERBACKS
For You to Enjoy

THE TROUBLE WITH ELEPHANTS
by Chris Riddell

Full of jolly jumbo jokes, this is a must for "elefans".

"Particularly likeable. It wittily records the many problems which can arise with elephants around,
such as their habit of eating all the buns at picnics and taking all the bedclothes at night." *The Sunday Times*

ISBN 0-7445-5447-0   £4.99

YOU'RE A HERO, DALEY B
by John Blake / Axel Scheffler

Daley B is a rabbit with an identity problem. He doesn't know who he is, where he should live or
what he should eat. But everything becomes only too clear when Jazzy D, the weasel, comes hunting.

"Charming, uncommonly funny book … green, prancing, spring-time pictures." *The Observer*

ISBN 0-7445-3158-6   £4.99

THE MAGIC BICYCLE
by Brian Patten / Arthur Robins

This rollicking round-the-world bike romp first appeared in a slightly different form,
in the classic poetry collection *Gargling with Jelly*.

"Packed with jokes and buzzing with life." *The Mail on Sunday*

ISBN 0-7445-3651-0   £4.99

Walker Paperbacks are available from most booksellers, or by post from B.B.C.S., P.O. Box 941, Hull, North Humberside HU1 3YQ

24 hour telephone credit card line 01482 224626

To order, send: Title, author, ISBN number and price for each book ordered, your full name and address,
cheque or postal order payable to BBCS for the total amount and allow the following for postage and packing:
UK and BFPO: £1.00 for the first book, and 50p for each additional book to a maximum of £3.50.
Overseas and Eire: £2.00 for the first book, £1.00 for the second and 50p for each additional book.
Prices and availability are subject to change without notice.